PIRATE SCHOOL
Ahoy, Ghost Ship Ahead!

by Brian James
illustrated by Jennifer Zivoin

Grosset & Dunlap

Visit us at www.abdopublishing.com

Reinforced library bound edition published in 2010 by Spotlight, a division of ABDO Group, 8000 West 78th Street, Edina, Minnesota 55439. This library bound edition is published by arrangement with Grosset & Dunlap, a member of Penguin Group (USA) Inc.

For my wife—and the ghost train we once encountered.—BJ

To my mom & dad, who have never stopped missing the ocean.—JZ

Library of Congress Cataloging-in-Publication Data
This title was previously cataloged with the following information:
James, Brian, 1976-
    Ahoy! ghost ship ahead / by Brian James ; illustrated by Jennifer Zivoin.
    p. cm. -- (Pirate School ; #2)
    Summary: While on lookout duty, the students of Pirate School spy a ghost ship following them, and when they bravely board it they receive a warning that may save their lives, if only they can convince Rotten Tooth or the captain that danger lies ahead.
    [1. Ghosts--Fiction. 2. Pirates--Fiction. 3. Schools--Fiction. 4. Adventure and adventurers--Fiction.] I. Title. II. Series.
PZ7.J153585 Cur 2007
[Fic]--dc22   2006038242

ISBN: 978-0-448-44625-7 (paperback)
ISBN: 978-1-59961-583-7 (reinforced library bound edition)

All Spotlight books have reinforced library binding and are manufactured in the United States of America.

Chapter 1
Rotten Trouble

The waves crashed against the side of the *Sea Rat*. The sky was dark, too. We were sailing right into a storm. The whole pirate ship rocked back and forth.

"Arrr! The sea is pretty rough today," I said. I held onto the mast to keep my balance. "This is going to be a big storm."

"Aye! It's making me a little seasick," Gary said, covering his mouth. His face was turning as green as the seaweed slop we'd had for breakfast.

"Blimey! Whoever heard of a pirate getting seasick?" Aaron asked. He held his gut and laughed. "A pirate getting seasick is like a bird being afraid of heights."

"Arrr! Stop teasing! You were seasick once, too!" Vicky snapped.

"Never!" Aaron bragged.

"Uh-huh!" Vicky argued. She's Aaron's twin sister. So she's known him every day of his entire life. "What about the time on our last ship when that seagull made an oops on your head? Then you made an oops all over the deck?"

Aaron's face turned red. He folded his arms and turned his back to us. "That was different," he said with a huff.

"Still counts." Vicky smiled, her dark eyes twinkling.

I looked at Gary. He still looked sickish. "Maybe you should go belowdecks."

"I'll be shipshape soon," he said. "I don't want to miss a single second of Pirate School. Besides, I think it's the seaweed slop that's making me sick."

"Aye!" I said. "That grub sure is gruesome."

It was Rotten Tooth's very own recipe. Good thing he wasn't always the cook. Rotten Tooth was the first mate. He was the meanest, dirtiest pirate on the ship. He only made his seaweed slop before storms. "It be good luck," he told us. He said it was a secret recipe. He should have said it was a *stinky* recipe.

But his cooking wasn't even the worst part about Rotten Tooth. The worst part was that he was also our pirate teacher! We had all come to this ship to go to Pirate School. But so far, Rotten Tooth hadn't taught us a thing!

"Where is Ol' Rotten Guts, anyway?" Aaron asked. "He's late for class!"

5

Just then, we saw Inna running up from the galley and onto the deck. As usual, she was wearing fancy clothes. Inna might not dress like a pirate, but that didn't mean she didn't want to become one.

"Arrr! Rotten Tooth's on his way," she shouted. Then she covered her mouth to hide a giggle. "He fell asleep with his face flat down in a bowl of slop!"

"Aye?" we asked.

"Aye!" Inna said. "And he blew bubbles in it when he snored!"

Then we all laughed.

"I wonder if that's the pirate lesson he'll teach us today," Vicky joked. "He'd probably tell Captain Stinky Beard that he was teaching us how to hold our breath and dive for sunken treasure!"

"Aye," I agreed.

Rotten Tooth always told the captain he was teaching us more than he was. One time, he told Captain Stinky Beard that he taught us how to wipe the deck clean of our enemies. He forgot to mention

6

the enemy was only grime and that our swords were mops. All he taught us was how to swab the deck. That's because Rotten Tooth didn't think kids could be good pirates. Lucky for us, Captain Stinky Beard was on our side.

"Yo-ho-ho!" Aaron said in his deepest voice. "I'm Rotten Face."

He pretended to walk around like Rotten Tooth. He stomped his feet and made grumbling noises.

"Pssst! Aaron?" Gary whispered, pointing his finger and trying to get Aaron to turn around.

Just then, a big hand came to rest on Aaron's head.

Aaron gulped! His dark eyes opened wide.

"AYE?" Rotten Tooth's voice boomed in our ears. "Then who be I?"

We looked up and saw Rotten Tooth's green teeth snarling at us. His face was covered with slop, and he looked meaner than ever!

"Uh . . . um," Aaron stuttered. He was frozen with fear.

"Arrr! Stop ye sniveling and fall in!" Rotten Tooth said.

"Aye aye!" Aaron said, and lined up with the rest of us.

We all stood as straight as we could. Rotten Tooth paced back and forth in front of us.

"Normally I'd make shark bait out of

anyone caught making fun of me," he said.

We all held our breath. I thought for sure he'd have us scrubbing dishes and washing decks for the rest of our days.

"But orders be orders. And my orders are to teach ye barnacles a lesson."

We weren't getting punished? I couldn't believe my ears.

"Aye?" I asked. I was too excited to stay quiet. "We're going to learn something today?" I couldn't wait for our first real pirate lesson.

"AYE! Ye will learn something," Rotten Tooth snarled. Then he leaned in close and laughed. His laughter boomed as loud as the thunder off the starboard bow. And the wind blew his stinky breath right into our faces.

Now I felt a little seasick. I held my nose. Something sure smelled rotten to me.

9

Chapter 2
From Sea to Stormy Sea

I held onto my pirate hat as the wind whipped around. "Arrr! It's really stormy up here in the crow's nest," I said, wiping the rain from my face.

"Aye!" Vicky agreed. Her normally reddish brown hair looked black. "How long did Rotten Tooth say we had to stay up here?"

Inna made a face. Then she squeezed the water out of her skirt. "Long enough to get completely soggy," she said. Then she looked at her hands and stuck her tongue out of her mouth. "My fingers are all wrinkly. YUCK!"

"Don't be such a pollywog," Aaron said. *Pollywog* was pirate speak for calling Inna a baby. "Besides, it's not so bad. The crow's nest is our secret hideout."

"AYE! But not when it's storming," Inna shouted and stomped her foot.

That was true. The crow's nest was our favorite spot on the ship. It's where we came to talk secret pirate kid things. But during a storm, it was always better to be warm and dry belowdecks.

"Aye," Gary said. "Soon it'll be our secret swimming pool."

I looked at my feet. The water was already up to my ankles. "Aye, we'd better use the bucket to bail out the water."

Gary picked up the bucket by his feet. He scooped up the water and tossed it over the side. But Gary didn't have very good aim. The bucket of water splashed right onto Vicky.

"Sink me!" Vicky said. "We're going to turn into fish up here."

"I think I'm already turning into a fish," Inna said, showing us her wrinkled hands again.

"Aye! Because *you* had to make fun of Rotten Tooth, *we* have to get all wet!" Vicky said, poking Aaron in the stomach.

"Blimey! It's not my fault Rotten Guts can't take a joke," Aaron said. "Besides, Gary got you all wet, not me."

Vicky was about to argue some more, but I interrupted.

"Avast! You're missing the most important part!" I finally said.

My friends all looked at me.

"Aye? What part?" Gary asked.

"The part about us finally getting our first real pirate duty," I answered. "We're the ship's lookouts!" I said proudly.

"But Rotten Tooth only sent us up here to get us out of the way," Aaron said.

"And to get back at us for your teasing," Vicky reminded Aaron.

"Aye," I agreed. "But he also told us to keep our eyes on the seas for rocks, reefs, and any other pirate ship that's being tossed by the storm. Being a lookout is a big job during a storm."

My friends all thought about what I'd said. Gary took off his glasses and rubbed his eyes. Inna put her finger up to her mouth. Aaron and Vicky squinted their eyes. That meant they were all thinking very hard.

"Pete's right," Vicky finally said. "Let's stop bellyaching and start doing our duty."

"Aye aye!" Gary agreed.

"Aye, we'll show Rotten Tooth that we're the best lookouts on the *Sea Rat*," Aaron said.

Inna frowned. She hated being soaking wet. "Aye," she mumbled. "I still wish he'd taught us something a little less soggy, though. But I'll do my best."

"That's the spirit, mateys!" I said. "A good pirate always tries to do the best he can."

Then I lifted the spyglass up to my eye and looked out to sea. I didn't see any rocks or reefs. I didn't see any other ships. "I only see waves," I said.

"Let me look," Aaron said.

I handed him the spyglass.

"Yep, nothing," he said.

Vicky took a turn next. She didn't see anything, either. Then she handed the spyglass to Gary.

Gary looked through it.

"ARRR!" Gary shouted. "A sea monster!"

Then Inna shouted, too.

We all ducked down to hide.

"If there's really a sea monster, it's our job to tell Captain Stinky Beard," I whispered.

"Aye, but first we better make sure it's a real sea monster," Vicky said.

"Aye!" I agreed. Sometimes Gary made mistakes. If we told the cap'n there was a sea monster when there wasn't, then the whole crew would think we were scallywags.

I stood up. Then I looked out to the sea. I didn't see any monsters.

I took the spyglass from Gary. Then I looked out again.

"Do you see it?" Gary asked.

"Aye," I said, and everyone gulped!

But then I showed them the end of the spyglass. There was a small piece of seaweed stuck to the lens.

"That's the sea monster?" Aaron asked.

I nodded. "It must have blown up here with the wind."

Gary shrugged his shoulders and smiled. "It looked scary through the lens," he said.

"Just wait until it makes its way into Rotten Tooth's slop." Vicky giggled. "Then it'll be *really* scary."

We all laughed. Then we went back to looking for the things we were told to look for. We also looked for mermaids. That was Inna's idea. "It's a true fact that mermaids love to swim in storms," she said.

But we didn't see any.

In fact, we didn't see anything.

The only things we saw were waves, waves, and more waves. But that was okay with me, because being a lookout sure beat scrubbing dishes!

Chapter 3
Soggy Report

By the time Rotten Tooth came back, it was raining even harder. We were soaked all the way through to our skivvies.

"Ahoy, all hands on deck," he shouted up to us.

We grabbed the ropes and swung down from the crow's nest.

My feet splashed down in a puddle on the main deck, and I gave Rotten Tooth a soggy salute.

Vicky landed next to me and did the same.

So did Aaron and Inna.

Gary did, too. Only Gary didn't really land on his feet. He landed splash-down on his butt.

"Lookout Pete reporting for duty!" I announced with a smile.

"Aye aye! Us too!" Vicky said for everyone else.

Rotten Tooth gave us all a long look. "Arrr! Why are ye mangy pups so sunny?" he sneered.

"Because!" I answered. "We completed our first real pirate duty."

Rotten Tooth roared with laughter. "Real pirate duty?" he said, shaking his head. Then he held his stomach and laughed some more.

We stopped smiling.

I put my head down. "Maybe being a

lookout isn't such an important job after all," I mumbled.

"Great sails! Lookout is one of the most important jobs on a ship," Captain Stinky Beard corrected, suddenly appearing behind us. "Especially during a storm," he added.

I popped up my head. Then I looked at Aaron and winked. "That's exactly what I said," I whispered to him.

Rotten Tooth had stopped laughing as soon as Captain Stinky Beard showed up. "Aye, Cap'n," he muttered. "I was just telling me little buckoes what a fine job they did."

Vicky rolled her eyes. "What a fibber," she muttered.

"Aye, a big stinky fibber," Inna whispered back.

Rotten Tooth glanced over at them and they quickly covered their mouths with both hands.

"Hmm," Captain Stinky Beard said. He gave Rotten Tooth a mean look. Then he looked back at us. "Well, what have ye to report?" he asked.

"Waves! Lots of them," I reported. I smiled extra wide. It was my first ever official report to the captain in my whole entire life. All nine years and three-quarters!

"Aye?" Captain Stinky Beard asked.

"AYE!" Gary shouted. "And water, too!"

We all giggled, even the captain.

"I'm proud of ye," he said. "It was mighty brave of ye to stay up there in a storm. Aye, Rotten Tooth?"

"Um . . . aye," Rotten Tooth stuttered.

"But it's getting dark, and the deck is no place for little shipmates during a storm," the captain said to us. "It's too dangerous.

That's why Rotten Tooth is taking your place as lookout until morning."

"Aye?" Rotten Tooth asked in surprise.

"Aye," the captain answered.

Rotten Tooth made a face and groaned. He looked up at the crow's nest. It was almost hidden by storm clouds. He gulped. Then he started to climb the rigging. "Aye," he mumbled, "orders be orders."

Then Captain Stinky Beard ordered us belowdecks for some grub.

"Not seaweed slop, I hope!" Gary said, turning a little green.

"No," Captain Stinky Beard said. "Only the best for me bravest pirates. Sardine ice cream for everyone!"

"HOORAY!" we cheered. Sardine ice cream is every pirate's favorite treat.

We hurried down the stairs. We dripped all the way into the kitchen.

"It feels good to be a pirate," Inna said, "even if it is a soggy job."

"Aye!" I said. "I couldn't have said it better myself!"

Chapter 4
Rise and Spook

The next morning, I woke up before the sun did. The *Sea Rat* creaked as I rubbed my eyes.

I looked out the porthole window.

"Arrr! Gary, the storm stopped," I said.

Gary answered with a snore.

I peeked over the side of my bunk. Gary was sound asleep in the bottom bunk. He used to have the top one, but he kept falling off in his sleep so we switched.

I looked around our quarters. Aaron and Vicky were asleep in their bunks, too. I couldn't see Inna. She had a pink curtain around her bed. But I could hear her snoring louder than anyone.

I picked up my spyglass as they slept.

I was still proud of the job we'd done the day before. I decided to give being a lookout another try. Now that the storm was over, maybe I'd see something besides waves.

I pointed the spyglass at the window and looked through.

"Waves," I mumbled.

I was about to put it down and go back to sleep when I spied something in the distance following the *Sea Rat*. I took a closer look.

I couldn't believe my eyes!

There was another ship following us. But it wasn't like any other ship I'd seen before. It looked like it was made of fog. It was all white and a little bit see-through.

"AVAST! A ghost ship!" I shouted as loud as I could. I'd heard plenty of stories about ghost ships before, but I never thought I'd see one. "Come look!" I shouted again. My friends needed to hurry. In every story, the ghost ship could only be seen in the dark. Once the sun came up, it'd be too late.

Aaron and Vicky sat right up in their bunks.

Inna pulled open the curtain around her bed.

Gary leaped awake, too. I felt his head THUMP against the bottom of my bed.

"A *what* ship?" Vicky asked.

"A *ghost* ship," I repeated, pointing out the porthole.

"Arrr! You were dreaming," Aaron said and put his head back down on the pillow.

"No way! I saw it!" I said. "A real live ghost ship. The sails looked like they were made of fog! So did the deck and the cabin! The whole thing was ghosty!"

Gary pressed his face to the window. "I don't see anything," he said.

"Aye?" I asked. I looked out the window and it was gone. Then I remembered something. "Oops!" I said. "I forgot the spyglass."

I looked out the window again. This time I used the spyglass. It was too far away to see without it.

There it was, a ghost ship sailing behind us.

I passed the spyglass to Gary.

"Avast! I see it, too!" he shouted. "I thought they only existed in old pirate tales."

"Aye! Me too," I said.

"Let me see!" Vicky said. She rushed over to our bunk. Gary gave her the spyglass.

"Shiver me timbers, it really is a ghost ship," Vicky said.

"Inna, don't you want to see it, too?" I asked.

Inna was still on her bed. She had her blanket pulled up over her head. "No way!" she said. "Ghosts are spooky and I don't like spooky things."

"It's not too spooky, I promise," I told her.

"Let me see it," Aaron whined. He tried

to grab the spyglass from Vicky.

She pulled it back.

"Wait your turn, greedy guts," Vicky said.

"It is my turn," he answered.

I rolled my eyes. Those two never got tired of arguing, not even when they just woke up.

Before Aaron got to look, Vicky started waving her arms around. "It's disappearing!" she shouted.

I took a look.

The ghost ship was becoming invisible.

"Why is it disappearing?" Vicky asked.

"Arrr! Maybe because there's no such thing!" Aaron said.

"Is too!" Vicky shouted at him.

"It's because the sun is rising," I said. "Ghosts don't like the sun. That's what the pirate stories say, anyway."

"Aye," Gary said. "The stories I've read said the same thing."

"But that still doesn't mean they're real," Aaron said.

Vicky rolled her eyes. Then she looked at me and Gary. "We need to find out why the ghost ship is following us. What does it mean?"

"Some pirates say they're good luck. But some say they're really bad luck," I said.

"Let's go find out what the pirates on *this* ship have to say about it," Gary suggested.

"Good idea. We can ask Rotten Tooth. Maybe he saw it, too," I said. "Rotten Tooth was standing watch all night. He had to have seen it."

"Aye aye!" everyone agreed.

We all rushed out of our quarters and headed for the deck.

Chapter 5
Whale of a Tale

Once we got to the main deck, I pointed up at the crow's nest. The pointy ends of Rotten Tooth's green beard were hanging over the side.

"I can hear him snoring from here," Inna said with a giggle.

I heard him, too. "He fell asleep on the job!" I shouted.

"What should we do?" Gary asked.

"Climb up there, that's what!" Vicky said.

"Aye!" I agreed. "We can't wait for him to wake up. Ghost ships are serious pirate business!"

We grabbed onto the ropes and started to climb.

When we reached the top, Rotten Tooth
was still asleep. And he was soaking wet!
The crow's nest was almost filled to the top
with rainwater.

"Sink me! It's like a swimming pool!"
Vicky said.

"You mean, sink him!" Aaron said.

"Aye." Inna laughed. "At least he finally
got a bath."

"Arrr," Rotten Tooth moaned as he
opened his eyes. "Be it morning already?"

"AYE!" we cheered.

Rotten Tooth covered his ears. "No need for shouting, mateys."

"Sorry," I said. "We're just excited. Know why?"

"Arrr, why?" he asked.

"Because I spied a ghost ship out at sea!" I yelled.

Rotten Tooth quickly covered his ears. "QUIET!" he yelled back. "I've been stuck up here all night because of ye barnacles! I'm not in the mood for any of ye whale tales!"

Whale tales was pirate speak for saying he didn't believe me.

"Aye, but it's true!" I said. "Didn't you see it while you were on lookout duty?"

"I'm not so sure he saw anything," Inna whispered. "It looks like he was on snoring duty."

Rotten Tooth growled.

Inna covered her mouth, but it was too late.

"I heard that," he said. I thought for

sure he was going to teach us another soggy lesson. But when Rotten Tooth opened his mouth to talk, all that came out was a big "A-CHOOO!"

His sneeze blew our hair back and filled the sails. I had to grab onto a rope to keep from falling.

"Now see what you did? Ye scurvy kids have caught me a cold." He sniffled. Then he stood up. His clothes dripped into the puddle at his feet. "School's closed today," he announced. "I be going belowdecks for some shut-eye."

"But what about the ghost ship?" I asked.

"Aye," Vicky said. "Don't we need to tell the cap'n?"

Rotten Tooth smiled as he began to climb down the rigging. "Aye, tell the cap'n. Ye will be doing me a favor," he said. "He'll laugh you right off the ship."

Rotten Tooth swung down to the deck without another word.

"But what're our orders for the day?" I hollered down.

"Arrr, your orders are to bother someone else!" Rotten Tooth hollered back. Then he entered the cabin and was out of sight.

"What should we do now?" Gary asked.

"We should try to find out more about that ghost ship," I said. "Three of us saw it. That means it has to be real."

"Aye, but how?" Vicky asked.

"We ask the one pirate on the *Sea Rat* who knows everything," I said.

"CLEGG!" Inna shouted.

Clegg was the oldest and wisest pirate onboard. Plus, he loved to tell us stories. He helped us figure out the curse of Snake Island before, and I was sure he could help us again.

"Let's go, buckoes!" I shouted. And we all headed off.

Chapter 6
Shipwrecked

We knew exactly where to find Clegg. He was always fishing off the back of the boat. "Maybe he spotted the ship, too," I said. "Let's hurry."

"Aye! I'll race you," Aaron challenged. Then he took off running. Aaron always wanted to race because he was the fastest.

Plus he liked to show off.

That always annoyed Vicky.

"Last one there's a rotten fish," he shouted.

"You run like a sea turtle," Vicky shouted back. "I'll beat you for sure." Then she took off running, too.

I tried to stop them. "The deck's too slippery!" I shouted, but they were already around the corner and out of sight.

Then we heard a CRASH!

Gary, Inna, and I all hurried to catch up. When we got to the very back of the ship, we saw Clegg holding Aaron's arm in one hand and Vicky's in the other.

"Ahoy! What happened?" I asked.

"Arrr, these little shipmates almost anchored themselves overboard," Clegg said with a smile.

"Aye, we slipped and tripped," Aaron said with a frown.

"No, *you* slipped and then tripped me," Vicky argued.

"'Tis okay with me," Clegg said. "You be the only fish I caught all morning."

Aaron and Vicky stopped arguing and laughed. In addition to knowing everything, Clegg was also one funny pirate!

I was still giggling when suddenly Inna nudged me. When I looked at her, she was pointing out to sea. "Ghosts, remember?" she whispered.

"Aye! I almost forgot," I said. We needed to find out about the ghost ship. "Clegg, have you been here all morning?" I asked.

"Aye. Even before the sun was up," he answered.

"And did you see anything sort of spooky?" I asked.

Clegg pointed to his eye patch. He only had one good eye. "I don't see much," he said with a wink.

We all frowned.

"So you didn't see a ghost ship?" I asked.

"Stormy seas! A ghost ship?" Clegg said with surprise. Then he shook his head slowly. "I haven't seen one of those for a hundred journeys."

"Saggy sails," I said, putting my head down. "Maybe it was a dream after all."

"Aye," Aaron said. "I told you. There's no such thing as ghost ships."

"I didn't say that, matey," Clegg corrected him. "I said I haven't seen one in a long time," he told us. Then he scratched his beard. He always did that before he was about to tell us a story.

"Then you saw one once?" I asked.

"Aye," Clegg answered.

We all made *ooohhhs* and *aaahhhs*. Even Aaron! Clegg never fibbed to us.

"What happened?" I asked.

"Well," Clegg began, "it was a stormy night and I couldn't sleep. I was looking out the porthole. Then all of a sudden, I spied a ghost ship out on the sea. And even in the storm, it was sailing calmly."

"Did you ever see it again?" Gary asked.

Clegg shook his head. "I only saw it once. The next night, our ship sank. I never saw another one."

"Blimey! A shipwreck!" Vicky said. "Did the ghost ship cause it?"

"It has to be bad luck, if it did," Gary added.

"Arrr . . . I don't know if the ghost ship caused it," Clegg answered. "But I do

know this. Ghost ships don't let everyone see them. The legends say they only show themselves to those they're willing to tell their secrets to."

We all gulped!

"There is a reason ye kids were the only mates to see it. Ye must find out what it wants. I wish I had. Perhaps me ship wouldn't have sank if I did."

"Yikes! That sounds like an important mission," I said. "Even more important than being the ship's lookouts."

"AYE!" my friends agreed.

"It is," Clegg said. "But I believe in ye."

We said good-bye to Clegg and headed off. We had a new pirate duty to perform.

Chapter 7
Sleepover Secrets

We stood in front of the main cabin ready to knock on the door. But nobody wanted to be the one to knock.

"What if Captain Stinky Beard is asleep?" Inna asked.

"Aye, no captain likes to get woken up," Vicky warned.

"Aye, he might fall off the bed and hit his head," Gary said. "That's what happens to me."

"But remember what Clegg told us? No one else saw the ship. That means it's up to us to find out if we're in danger," I said. "What if the ghost ship causes the *Sea Rat* to sink?"

"There's only one way to find out,"

Aaron said. He picked up a fishing pole and swung it around like a sword. "We wait for that ghost ship tonight and find a way to make those ghosts tell us what they want."

We all ducked as the fishing pole swung over our heads.

"Aye," I said. "That's why we need the captain's permission to let us sleep on the deck. Then if it comes again, we can signal it and see what it wants."

We had to duck again as Aaron turned around. The pole swung over us. But Gary was too slow and got whacked on the head.

"Ouch!" he yelled. "Why did you hit me? I'm not a ghost."

"Sorry," Aaron mumbled.

"We won't need swords. I don't think they work on ghosts, anyway," I said. I took the fishing pole out of his hands. It was a good thing no pirate ever gave Aaron a real sword. He'd be the most dangerous pirate on the sea.

"Now let's go, mates," I continued. "We need to ask the captain . . ."

"Ask me what?" a voice boomed from behind us.

We were so startled that we jumped in the air. Captain Stinky Beard must have been on deck the whole time.

"Ahoy, Cap'n," I said with a salute.

He saluted back. "What were you brave little pirates talking about? It sounded important."

"Um . . . um," I stuttered. I couldn't think of anything to say. I looked at Vicky and Aaron. They couldn't think of anything, either.

"Um, we were talking about a sleepover," Inna said. "We thought it would be good pirating if we slept on deck. That way, we could take turns being lookout all night."

Captain Stinky Beard scratched his head. "Sounds like a right smart idea," he said.

Inna smiled. She sure was a clever pirate.

"Aye, I grant you permission!" Captain Stinky Beard said.

We were all so excited that we gave our pirate cheer.

"SWASHBUCKLING, SAILING, FINDING TREASURE, TOO!

"BECOMING PIRATES IS WHAT WE WANT TO DO!"

Captain Stinky Beard smiled. "Rotten Tooth sure has done a fine job teaching ye kids to take your duty seriously."

"Aye! If our duty was snoring," Vicky whispered to me.

I covered my mouth to keep from

giggling. It was not polite to giggle in front of the captain. That's a pirate rule. I learned that before I ever even came to Pirate School.

Then Captain Stinky Beard thought of something. "You won't be too afraid of the dark, will you?" he asked Inna. He knew Inna liked to keep a lantern on at night. She did not like the dark. It made her a little bit afraid.

But Inna smiled bravely. "No," she lied. "I won't be afraid of the dark."

"Aye, that's a good pirate," the captain

said. "I must be heading inside now to look at some maps," he continued. "That storm blew us off course. Have a jolly time on your sleepover."

As soon as we were alone again, I gave Inna a thumbs-up.

"Good job!" I said. "That was fast thinking."

"Aye," Gary said. "But I thought you were afraid of the dark."

"I am," Inna said. "But I won't be afraid of the dark tonight, because I'll be too busy being afraid of ghosts."

Chapter 8
BOO!

Once the sun set, we grabbed our blankets and raced up on deck. On the way, we ran into Rotten Tooth. He was still sneezing and sniffling.

"ARRR!" he growled. "Where do ye pollywogs think you be going?"

"On deck," I answered. "The captain said we could have a sleepover."

Rotten Tooth made a face. But if Captain Stinky Beard said we could, there was nothing he could do. "Aye? You're going to sleep here all night?" he asked.

"Aye!" Gary said. "We're going to look out for the ghost ship."

We all turned our heads.

Gary covered his mouth. "It slipped," he said.

"Ghost ship?" Rotten Tooth laughed.

"Aye," Aaron said bravely. "And we're going to catch one of those ghosts."

Rotten Tooth laughed harder. Then he sneezed again. "The only thing ye will catch is a cold."

I folded my arms and made a huff. We'd show him!

"Come on, let's go!" I said. Then we all marched past him. We could still hear him laughing and sneezing as we set up our blankets for the night.

But soon, everything was quiet. And once it got dark, the crew of the *Sea Rat* was sound asleep.

We kept watch. We all took turns looking through the spyglass, but all we saw were waves. Inna didn't even see those. She stayed hidden under her blanket.

"Maybe it won't come if we're not asleep," Gary said.

"Aye," Vicky agreed. "We should close our eyes."

"Aye," Gary said with a yawn.

"ARRR!" Aaron said, "If we close our eyes, we won't see it at all."

"I don't want to see it, anyway," Inna said, peeking out from under her blanket.

"That's because you are a scallywag," Aaron teased.

"Am not! I just don't like spooky stuff,"

Inna said. "Especially in the dark."

As they argued, I kept looking. It seemed really foggy at sea. Then I took a closer look at the fog. It had the shape of a ship. I could see three tall masts and three giant sails.

"BLOW ME DOWN!" I hollered. "Ghost ship, dead ahead!"

"You mean dead behind," Vicky said. Then she laughed, because "behind" was a funny word.

"Will everyone stop saying *dead*?" Inna said.

"Aye, good idea," I said, because "dead" was one spooky word.

Aaron peered through the spyglass. "Avast, it's real . . . and it's getting closer!"

I took another look.

He was right. The ghost ship was sailing much faster than the *Sea Rat*. In fact, it was the fastest ship I'd ever seen. It seemed to float over the waves.

It was amazing! My mouth fell open as the ghost ship caught up to us. In no time at all, it was sailing right beside us!

Chapter 9
All Aboard!

A ghost plank stuck out from the ship and touched the deck of the *Sea Rat*. "Shiver me timbers!" I said, staring down at it. I thought for sure a ghost was going to come aboard.

We waited, but no ghosts showed up.

"Maybe we should go investigate," I suggested.

"Do you think it's safe?" Vicky asked.

"Aye? What if we turn into ghosts?" Gary asked.

"That's silly," Aaron said with a snort.

"That's what you said about ghost ships!" Vicky said.

"So I was wrong." Aaron shrugged.

"Well, we have to find out," I said. "It's

rude not to go aboard when another pirate ship lowers a plank. That's in the pirate code." My friends were lucky to have a mate like me. I knew all about the pirate code.

"Aye! But that's not a pirate ship, it's a ghost ship!" Inna said.

"But it's a *pirate* ghost ship," I said, pointing to the pirate flag on the mast. "Ghosts or no ghosts, we have to follow the pirate code."

I didn't wait for an answer. I took a step onto the plank. I was a little afraid that I would fall right through. But I didn't.

Once I was on the deck of the ghost ship, I reached down and touched it. "It feels funny. It's sort of like a spiderweb," I said.

"Cool!" Vicky said. "Let's check it out."

"Aye aye!" Aaron and Gary agreed.

Inna was the only one who wasn't excited. "I hate spiders just as much as ghosts," she said. But finally she ran across the plank.

I looked all around. I spied the cabin and the crow's nest. Then I spied the fish tank.

It all looked very familiar. "Arrr," I said.
"Does anyone else notice something fishy
about this ship?"

"Aye!" Inna said, lifting her foot. She
made a face at the stuff that was stuck to
her shoes. "It's not just spooky, it's super
gross, too!"

"Not that!" I said. "I mean, it looks just
like the *Sea Rat*, only ghosty."

"Aye!" Vicky said, looking around.
"Pete's right. It's the same ship."

"But where's the crew?" Gary asked.

"If it's just like the *Sea Rat*, then the
crew must be sleeping," I said.

"Then how are we supposed to find out what it's trying to tell us?" Aaron asked.

All of a sudden, Inna gulped!

"Aye, I think they'll tell us," she said. Then she covered her eyes with one hand and pointed behind us with the other.

I spun around.

I couldn't believe my eyes. On the other side of the deck were five ghost kids who looked just like us!

"YIKES!" Gary screamed. "I knew this was going to be trouble."

And for once, Gary was right. I was beginning to think we were in big ghosty trouble!

My timbers were shaking and shivering. So were all of my friends'. Even Aaron didn't seem so brave anymore.

"Ahoy," I said, a little bit afraid.

Then the ghost who looked like me said, "Ahoy right back!"

All five of the ghost kids came right up to us. We all stared at the ghosts. They were just like us, only see-through.

I tried my best to be brave.

"Who are you?" I asked. "And why do you look like us?"

"We're ghosts," they answered. "And ghosts can be spooky. So we made ourselves look like you so you wouldn't be scared."

Inna poked Aaron in the side. "See, I told you ghosts were spooky! Even they say so!"

Aaron made a face. "I'm not scared," he said. "And I don't think *he* looks anything like me!"

The ghost Aaron made a face, too. "Aye, I look better," he said. Both Vickys rolled their eyes. Aaron was a show-off even as a ghost.

And Gary's ghost was just as clumsy! When he went to shake Gary's hand, his foot got caught on a ghost rope. He tumbled onto the deck. Then Gary tumbled on top of him trying to help him up.

We all laughed, even the ghosts.

But then I remembered the story about Clegg's shipwreck. We might still be in danger. So I took a deep breath and got my courage up.

"Why did you sail up next to us?" I asked. "Are you going to sink our ship?"

The ghosts looked surprised.

"Blimey! Never!" they answered. "Ghost ships follow other ships to warn them of danger. Those who are brave enough to board our ship are saved."

"Aye?" we asked.

"AYE!" they answered. "The *Sea Rat* was blown off course in the storm. You're heading straight for Dead Man's Rocks! You need to change course or ye will be shipwrecked."

"Shiver me timbers!" I hollered. Dead Man's Rocks had sunk hundreds of ships. Every sailor knew to steer clear of them. "We need to warn Captain Stinky Beard!"

"Aye," the ghosts said. "And hurry!"

We thanked the ghosts and waved good-bye. Then we all ran as fast as we could back to our ship.

The ghost ship disappeared as soon as we were safely aboard the *Sea Rat*.

Chapter 10
Gangway!

"All hands on deck! All hands on deck!" we shouted as loudly as we could.

Rotten Tooth was the first pirate to rush up from the galley. Gary didn't see him. He ran right into Rotten Tooth and they both landed with a CRASH!

"All hands on deck!" I shouted even louder than before.

Then Rotten Tooth stood up and quickly covered my mouth. "QUIET!" he yelled. "Ye screaming sea dogs could wake the sun with all that racket!"

"Sorry," I mumbled. "But this is very, very, *very* important."

"Aye!" Inna shouted. "We went aboard the ghost ship! And there were ghosts that looked just like us!"

"Aye! They even acted like us," Gary added, rubbing his arm where he fell on top of his ghost.

"Arrr!" Rotten Tooth growled, showing his pointy green teeth. "Not another whale of a tale about ghosts," he said. "I knew letting ye kids spend the night up here was a bad idea. Ye are all spooked by the dark."

"It's not a tale!" I said, stomping my foot. "It was real. They said we were heading for Dead Man's Rocks and that we were going to sink!" I shouted.

"Dead Man's Rocks? That be a day's journey from here," Rotten Tooth snarled.

"But they said we were blown off course," Inna said.

"Aye! And the captain said that, too," Vicky added.

Rotten Tooth still didn't believe us. "Then where be your ghost ship now?" he asked with a smirk.

"It disappeared," Inna answered.

"Aye? Of course it did," Rotten Tooth said.

"It really did," Gary pleaded. But Rotten
Tooth wouldn't listen. He grabbed my arm
and Inna's. Then he grabbed Gary's. But
Aaron and Vicky were too quick. They
rushed away and headed straight for the
crow's nest.

"Where are ye going?" Rotten Tooth shouted.

"To look out for rocks," Vicky cried out as she kept climbing the ropes.

"I order ye down here, and straight off to bed," Rotten Tooth hollered. Aaron gave a quick glance down and stuck out his tongue.

Soon most of the crew was on the deck. Rotten Tooth got madder than I'd ever seen him. If those ghosts weren't right, we were all going to get thrown out of Pirate School!

"What's going on?" Captain Stinky Beard asked, coming out of his quarters.

"Arrr, 'tis nothing, sir," Rotten Tooth said. "Just these kids acting up again. I warned ye this Pirate School idea was trouble."

Captain Stinky Beard gave me a stern look. "What have ye got to say?" he asked.

"Cap'n, we saw a ghost ship! It told us to change course or we'd sink, but Rotten Tooth doesn't believe us!" I said.

Inna and Gary nodded their heads.

Captain Stinky Beard's expression changed right away. "Did you say you saw a ghost ship?" he asked.

"Aye!" I answered.

Before I could say anything else, the captain ordered Rotten Tooth to let us go. Then he turned to the crew. "All hands man the sails!" he shouted.

"Cap'n? You don't believe them, do ye?" Rotten Tooth asked. "It's just a story."

Then Captain Stinky Beard gave him a stern look. It was even more stern than the look he'd given me. "Perhaps you need to go back to Pirate School," he said. "Any good pirate should know a ghost ship sighting is a sign of danger."

"AVAST! Dead Man's Rocks ahead!" Aaron and Vicky shouted down to us.

"Turn the ship!" Captain Stinky Beard ordered, and the crew pulled on the ropes.

The sails swung around. The wind quickly filled them. And the *Sea Rat* began to turn toward safety.

The whole crew cheered.

Rotten Tooth looked over the port side. Jagged rocks rose above the waves. "One second longer, and those rocks would have sank our ship," Captain Stinky Beard said to him.

I looked up at Rotten Tooth. He looked down at me. "At least then I wouldn't have to teach ye mangy kids anymore," he mumbled.

"Aye, and we wouldn't have to eat his seaweed slop!" I whispered to Inna and Gary. Then we all started laughing.

Aaron and Vicky swung down from the crow's nest. Captain Stinky Beard ordered the whole crew to gather around us.

"Three cheers for our little shipmates," he said. "Lucky for us, they are brave young pirates who take their duty seriously." Then he flashed Rotten Tooth a look. That look meant Rotten Tooth needed to take his duty more seriously.

"Hip-hip hooray! Our little shipmates saved the day!" the crew cheered three times.

We all smiled as wide as we could. We'd passed this lesson with flying colors.

I couldn't wait for our next lesson at Pirate School.